Date: 2/17/16

LAC J MACGREGOR
MacGregor, Cynthia,
Heartfelt, the special reindeer /

This Book Belongs To:

_____

Heartfelt, the Special Reindeer

by Cynthia MacGregor
illustrations by Verónica Rosado

Acknowledgments

I would like to thank Michel Marion,
who believes in my dream for this book almost as fiercely as I do
and agreed to bring it to life.

And Lawrence Rein,
who wrote the music for the song "It's Heartfelt"
as well as providing the vocals and instrumentals
for the recording

Copyright© 2015 by Cynthia MacGregor
AcuteByDesign Publishing
ISBN 978-1-943515-94-3

ACUTE BY DESIGN

the little book company that could

AcuteByDesign is a teeny, tiny book publishing
company with a big mission:

To produce and publish high quality diverse,
multicultural, and socially relevant
books for children and young readers;
their teachers, and parents

To provide opportunities for teachers and
under-represented writers and illustrators to
publish their dream book, and

To provide small grants to teachers and
parent associations to help provide resources
for underserved students and classrooms.

Thank you for helping to make that dream come true for so many!

www.acutebydesign.com

Use this link to download a FREE copy
of the song "It's Heartfelt" to play on
any of your devices whenever you want!

https://www.reverbnation.com/lawrencerein/song/24076739-its-heartfelt

Dedication

For all children everywhere,
and for all adults who have kept alive the child in them
and not lost the power to believe

The North Pole is an icy cold place in the middle of December, but reindeer don't mind the chill at all. Their fur keeps them nice and warm. Blitzen was aiming snowballs at Dasher's antlers, while Rudolph and Vixen built a snow fort. They invited Prancer to help them, but Prancer shrugged and walked away.

"What's bugging her?" Dancer wondered aloud.

"She misses her mom," said Heartfelt.

Heartfelt was one of Santa's "backup reindeer," who are there in case one of the nine regular reindeer isn't able to pull his sleigh on Christmas Eve.

Heartfelt wanted nothing more in this world than to be part of Santa's team. It was her heartfelt wish.

Prancer's heartfelt wish right now was to go home and visit her mom. Her mom lived with a group of other reindeer, far from Santa's workshop. But this close to Christmas all Santa's reindeer had to stick around the North Pole and be ready to fly. And meanwhile, they had to rest up and be ready for Christmas Eve.

"How do you know Prancer misses her mom?" Dancer asked Heartfelt.

"I know it in here," Heartfelt said, touching one hoof to her heart.

Dancer nodded. She knew that Heartfelt had a special gift, the ability to feel what other people's heartfelt wishes were.

Heartfelt was "special" in another way, too: Her two back legs were shorter than her front legs. When she walked, she wobbled. The other reindeer never laughed. They had learned that it isn't nice to laugh at someone just because they're different.

However, Heartfelt could fly every bit as well, every bit as far, and every bit as fast as any of Santa's other reindeer.

Heartfelt went to look for Prancer, who had wandered away from the group. Heartfelt wobbled her way past a nearby snowbank and found Prancer sitting on the other side of it.

"Christmas is in just a couple of weeks," Heartfelt said. "You'll be able to go see your mom after that." Secretly she wished Prancer could go see her mom *now*. Then maybe Heartfelt could take Prancer's place and finally get a chance to help pulling Santa's sleigh on Christmas Eve. Then everyone would be happy.

"Thanks," Prancer said. "That's a nice thought. It's something to look forward to."

Just then Santa hurried out of his workshop and went into a shed nearby. He came out carrying an armload of hay and a handful of carrots to feed the reindeer.

"I want all of you to be strong and healthy for Christmas Eve," he said as he spread out the hay and carrots. "Eat plenty. You backup reindeer, too. You never know when I'll need one of you."

"Oh, I wish…!" Heartfelt thought. "I wish you would need me this year."

Santa turned around and hurried back to his workshop. After all, this was his busiest time of the year. It was nearly Christmas. But he didn't let out a single "Ho-ho-ho."

Blitzen looked up from the hay he was munching on and whispered to the others, "Did you notice Santa didn't laugh? Not one Ho-ho-ho."

"I noticed," said Comet. "He looked very serious. I wonder what's bothering him?"

The reindeer picked their heads up from their food and looked at Heartfelt. They all knew that Heartfelt had a special gift; she could see into the hearts of others. Vixen asked, "Why is Santa so sad?"

Heartfelt's eyes took on the faraway, dreamy look she got when she was reading someone's heart. She reached out to Santa's heart with her own. Then she said, "There's a little boy named James who is very sad and crying a lot, but Santa hasn't figured out why yet. Santa would like to bring James what he wants for Christmas, but James hasn't sent Santa his list. It's bothering Santa that he doesn't know how to make James happy."

"Don't *you* know what James wants?" Comet asked. "What's his most heartfelt wish?"

"I wish I knew!" Heartfelt said. "But James lives too far away for my heart to reach out to his heart from here."

By and by, it got to be bedtime. The reindeer bedded down for the night in their stable.

It was only a few short days till Christmas Eve, and Heartfelt continued to dream of helping pull Santa's sleigh through the air on the most important night of the year.

The morning before Christmas Eve, Santa and his elves got up extra early and started packing the sleigh. This year there were more heavy presents than usual. Dolls, stuffed animals, and video games don't weigh that much and they were usually the most requested presents. But this year, more kids than usual had asked for bikes, sleds and other heavy gifts.

It was late in the afternoon, almost time to take off. Suddenly an elf waving a calculator shouted, "Santa! Santa! We've got a problem. A huge problem!"

"What is it?" Santa asked. He immediately grew concerned.

"The reindeer aren't going to be able to pull the sleigh this year. It's too heavy! I've been doing some calculations, and we don't have enough reindeer power to get the sleigh off the ground!"

"Not even with all nine reindeer?" Santa asked, frowning.

"It's still not enough!" the elf said. "I put all the numbers into the calculator. The weight of all the presents. The strength of the reindeer. Everything. You just aren't going to be able to do it, Santa!"

Santa stroked his white beard and cautiously asked the elf, "What if we add another reindeer? One of the backups?"

The elf punched some numbers into his calculator. "Yes! Yes! That could work!" he shouted.

"Well, get the other elves to help you with the extra harness. We fly ten reindeer tonight for the first time in history."

But who would the tenth reindeer be? There were several extremely strong reindeer among the backups. Santa looked up to where the nine regular team members were pacing around. They were eager to get going on their yearly trip around the world, delivering presents to all the good girls and boys.

Two of the biggest, strongest backup reindeer were standing nearby. Heartfelt's head drooped low to the ground. She wanted so badly to be the tenth member of the team. But she was sure Santa would pick one of the bigger, stronger reindeer. Tears began to leak from Heartfelt's eyes. But as Santa approached the two big, strong reindeer, Heartfelt spoke up. She wanted so badly to fly with the team. And she would not lose her opportunity without trying.

"I can do it, Santa!" she said eagerly. "Let me be your tenth team member tonight."

Santa looked her over. Her back sloped down because of her short rear legs. She wobbled as she stood there. But Santa knew that Heartfelt was a strong flyer. "You want to be part of the team tonight?" Santa asked her. "You want to be the tenth reindeer, just for this year? Have you been resting and eating well? Are you feeling strong and ready?"

Heartfelt leaped up into the air in her excitement. When she landed, she wobbled, but she stayed on her feet. "Ready and eager to help!" she answered.

"Good!" said Santa. "We'll leave in half an hour."

Heartfelt hurried to share the news with the other nine team members. "I'm going with you guys this year!" she told them excitedly. "Santa needs me!"

Even with ten reindeer pulling the sleigh, they barely managed to get it off the ground. It was just that overloaded with toys, games, and other presents. But with the added strength of Heartfelt, they got the sleigh up in the air and kept it flying. They had to deliver those presents!

When they got close to the town where James lived, Santa sighed heavily. He knew that James had been a very good boy that year. But he still hadn't sent Santa his list, so Santa didn't know what James wanted for Christmas—or what he was so sad about.

As they got closer to James's house, however, Heartfelt was able to pick up on the special wish that was in James's heart. His puppy, Brownie, had run away, and James and his parents had been unable to find him. What James wanted more than anything else in the world was to get his puppy back.

The reindeer kept swooping down to rooftop after rooftop, and Santa delivered presents and more presents and still more presents. Then they flew across a park. Suddenly Heartfelt's heart picked up some strong signals. "Wait! Stop! Land here!" she called out to the other team members.

The nine other reindeer hesitated. Why did Heartfelt want to land the sleigh here? Dasher was next to Heartfelt in the harness. He said, "There aren't any homes here. It's just a park." He thought the newest team member was making a mistake.

"Land! We have to land here!" Heartfelt said urgently.

She was so insistent that the reindeer listened and flew down to land in the park.

"What's going on?" asked Santa. "Why did you stop?"

"It's James's puppy, Brownie!" Heartfelt said. "His lost puppy. He's around here somewhere. That's all James wants for Christmas—to get Brownie back. My heart is picking up both of their signals—James's and the puppy's. We're near the puppy."

Santa got out of the sleigh and looked around. "There's nothing here but an old cardboard box next to that trash can. I don't see a puppy. Let's go! We'll be late delivering our presents," he warned.

"Look in the box—please!" Heartfelt begged. Her heart was picking up very strong signals from James's Brownie.

Santa looked inside the box. And there, curled up and shivering, he saw a small, cold, scared ball of brown fur. He picked up the shivering pup and held him close to the warmth of his red velvet coat. "Are you James's dog?" he gently asked.

Of course the dog couldn't answer, but Heartfelt did. "Yes! That's James's puppy, Brownie. He's lost, but his most heartfelt wish is to go home to James."

"Then we'll have to take him, won't we?" Santa said. After picking up the puppy, Santa climbed back into the sleigh. "Change the route!" Santa called out to the reindeer. "Go straight to James's house. And don't land on the roof. Land on the front lawn. I can't take the puppy down the chimney."

When Santa rang the doorbell, James was in bed, crying, and his parents were asleep. They didn't hear the doorbell. They didn't hear James crying, either.-

Santa rang again. James got out of bed and went downstairs to answer the door himself. He put the chain lock in place before he opened the door.

When he looked through the safety chain, he was very surprised to see Santa Claus at his front door. And he was even more surprised when he saw what Santa was holding. His puppy! "Brownie!" he squealed. He unhooked the chain and threw the door open.

"I have a special delivery for you, James," Santa said as he handed the puppy over to the boy. Brownie wriggled and licked James's face all over. Santa couldn't tell who was happier, James or Brownie.

Santa was very happy, too. He had been able to bring James what he wanted most, thanks to Heartfelt. James looked up from hugging his puppy. "Thank you , Santa," he said. His face was all wet, but this time it was from puppy kisses, not tears.

"Merry Christmas!" Santa said with a huge smile. Then he turned around to get back in his sleigh. "Ho-ho-ho!" he said. "Up we go, reindeer. Up we go. Let's finish our deliveries."

It was a long and busy night, but finish they did.

Back at the North Pole, as the reindeer got out of their harnesses, the other nine all congratulated Heartfelt. "Good job!" they told her, "Well done," and "We're glad you came along this year."

Just then, Santa came looking for the special reindeer with the short back legs and the special ability. "I don't know what we would have done without you tonight," Santa told her. "You gave us the added strength we needed to pull the sleigh. You read James's heart and found his puppy. You not only saved Christmas for James, you saved it for me, too. Would you like to be a regular member of the team? We may not have as heavy a load to carry next year. But you have a special talent. I want you along with the others every year from now on."

"Oh, thank you!" Heartfelt exclaimed.

And that's how Heartfelt's own heartfelt wish came true.

So next year, if you happen to be lucky enough to see Santa when he flies through the sky on Christmas Eve, you might notice that there are ten reindeer pulling the sleigh now. There are Dasher, Dancer, Prancer, Vixen, Comet, Cupid, Donner, Blitzen, Rudolph—and Heartfelt, the special reindeer with the special ability. She's the happiest member of Santa's team!

Peacefully

The End

Prolific author Cynthia MacGregor has written over 100 fiction and nonfiction books for both children and adults, more information on which can be found on her website, www.cynthiamacgregor.com.

She has produced and hosted two TV shows, *Solo Parenting* and *Younger Every Day*, both of which aired on WHDT in the South Florida viewing area. She was the number-two finalist one year at the O. Henry Pun-Off World Championships, an annual wordplay competition, where more recently she has been tapped to be one of the judges.

After having several of her books accepted for publication by AcuteByDesign, Cyn (as she likes to be called) agreed to be part of the AbyD "team," serving in editorial and other capacities.

Cynthia absolutely loves her work, and she is emphatic when she says, "I can't wait to bound out of bed in the mornings and get started. I might be the happiest person in the world. There's no one in the world I'd want to trade lives with."

Also by this author:

Moving Day for Alex

Octopus Pie

Ants in His Pants

...and many others

You can get in touch with Cynthia at
cynthia@cynthiamacgregor.com

CPSIA information can be obtained
at www.ICGtesting.com
Printed in the USA
LVOW01*2233211115
463365LV00024B/267/P

9 781943 515943